BE MIGHTY!

Kendra Ocampo
CVO ☺

# MIGHTY MAY
## WON'T CRY TODAY

By **Kendra & Claire-Voe Ocampo**

Illustrated by **Erica De Chavez**

Bunny Patch Press

In a house on a hill,
just outside Sunnyville,
a little but mighty girl named May
deeply dreams of her first school day.

Sunlight bursts in.
May is wide awake.
She leaps from bed.
She can't be late.
Adventures ahead!
Adventures await!

Bright yellow school bus stretches long and tall. Clouds swell above.

Drip, drip, drip.

Rain drops fall.

May kisses Mommy and Mama.
Good-bye!
She's excited, she's nervous—
but she WILL NOT cry.

May feels uncertain.
Her heart beats
*Da dum da dum da dum.*

She hears the bus
*Hum hum hum.*

"Don't worry, May,
come sit next to me.
Cheer up, I'm here!"
Troy calls eagerly.

May nods.

May sits.

May waits.

The bus rolls on.
When the bus stops,
the rain is gone!

SUNNYVILLE
ELEMENTARY

Ring ring ring!
May is here at last.
The school bell chimes.
She must hurry fast.

Zigzag,

Zoom,

down the hallway
to the room.

Teetering,

Toppling,

BooM!

May closes her eyes.
She must try.
She breathes.
She counts.
She WILL NOT cry.

1-2-3-4-5-

"I'm here!" May announces
with a smile and a wiggle.
Her classmates laugh.
They clap and they giggle.

"Wow, what an entrance!"
says her teacher, Mr. Finn.
"Quiet down and gather 'round.
It's time to begin."

Art class, May's favorite.
Blues and yellows whirl.
swoosh, swoosh, swoosh.
Reds and greens swirl.

The sun, the sky,
clouds here and there—
paint is everywhere!

May adds some trees,
a bird and a plane.
Her lucky skirt, *oh no!*
An embarrassing stain!

May sighs.
What a mess!
May's eyes become wet.
Mr. Finn leans in.
"May, don't give up yet!"

May gets an idea . . .

May's idea blooms—a colorful one.

Splashes of paint on her skirt—what fun!

Voilà, a flower masterpiece!
She's done.

May's stomach growls.
Rumble, rumble, rumble.
She races to lunch.
Grumble, grumble, grumble.
Mommy packed cheese.
Mama packed peas.
Munch, munch, munch.
May is pleased.

May digs.
May blinks,
her face
bright pink.

"Oh no, I forgot
my smoothie to drink!"

May's first day speeds by.
She is happy with pride.
May feels brave, strong.
She never cried.

Houses, trees,
and people outside.
Up down, up down,
a long, bumpy ride.

*I missed my stop.*
*Where should I go?*
*How will I get home?*
*Am I all alone?*

May bursts into tears.

Rushing, gushing, soaking her shirt.
Flowing, flooding, down to her skirt.
May's heart sinks.

What will Mama and Mommy think?

"Don't be scared, May.
It will all be OK."
Miss Rose comforts.
"I know the way."

"Mama and Mommy, I'm home!"
With warm, nuzzling hugs,
Moms are curious to know,
May tells her story,
every high, every low.

HOME

Then, Mama grins
and Mommy too.

"May, it's OK to cry."

"We all do."

May looks up, surprised.
*Could it be true?*

Mama's first time skating.
"I was falling and crying.
I could have quit then,
but thanks to Mommy
I tried again."

1st Date

Mommy talks about Chew—
"Remember that time
he ate my shoe?"
"Yes, I miss him so much."
"And we do too."

Mommy shows a photo.
Two sparkling gowns.
Mommy and Mama tearful,
exchanging wedding vows.
"It's your wedding!"

Two mommies cuddle
a newborn baby.
May looks closer
and exclaims "That's me!"
"Yes, a very special day,
the first of May!"

"Let's capture today's adventure,
learning it's OK to shed a tear.
It's part of our emotions,
sadness, joy, frustration, fear."

"Crying helps us show each other
what we need and how we feel.
It teaches us to reach out.
It teaches us to heal."

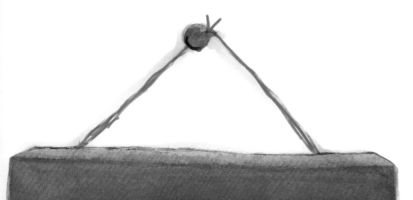

In a house on a hill,
just outside Sunnyville,
the sun slips down.
The day is done.

A big and fearless girl
confidently dreams
of what she'll overcome.

for xiomara, our little bookworm

for violet, born on a special day in may

Publisher's Cataloging-in-Publication Data

Ocampo, Kendra, author. | Ocampo, Claire-Voe, author. | De Chavez, Erica, illustrator. Mighty May won't cry today / by Kendra & Claire-Voe Ocampo ; illustrated by Erica De Chavez. Edison, NJ: Bunny Patch Press, 2020. | Summary: An imaginative and determined May tries not to shed a tear on her first day of school, but with the help of her two moms learns why it's okay to cry. LCCN 2019915328 | ISBN 978-1-7341112-0-0 (hardcover) | 978-1-7341112-2-4 (pbk.) | 978-1-7341112-1-7 (ebook). LCSH First day of school—Juvenile fiction. | Crying—Juvenile fiction. | Family life—Juvenile fiction. | Lesbian mothers—Juvenile fiction.| Mothers and daughters—Juvenile fiction. | CYAC First day of school—Fiction. | Crying—Fiction. | Family life—Fiction. | Lesbian mothers—Fiction. | BISAC: JUVENILE FICTION / Social Themes / Emotions & Feelings | JUVENILE FICTION / LGBT | JUVENILE FICTION / Family / Alternative Family

LCC PZ7.1 .O197 Mi 2019 | DDC [E]--dc23